VOLUME #2

First paperback edition January 2023

Book design by Andrew Rogers

ISBN 979-8-9872560-2-2 (paperback)
ISBN 979-8-9872560-3-9 (ebook)

www.sanchicatalina.com

Sanchi Catalina Volume 2 / Andrew Rogers --1st ed.

Chapters

OS 12
PST 56
SOLARIS F23
DN 0084S2231
DN 0084S2232
DN 0034228Z

Chapter 13

Viviana's Diary

Page 3 Leaving this Awful Planet

It took a while for me to fall asleep on that bumpy train ride. I'm so far away from my home and know nothing about this place. Maybe it was being around these strange women that made me comfortable to fall asleep. Feeling a long curve on the ride, I woke up,

realizing I wasn't home in my bed. Looking around,
I could see that most were still asleep, except for Jasi
and Tatiana. They still blacked the windows out, and
I couldn't tell if it was night or day. Jasi was still in a
deep thought about what was going on, while Tatiana

worked on a small computer device. She noticed me awake and said we had a little longer until we got to the spaceport. The planet that we will depart to is a place called Garbon. There will be an enormous crowd at the spaceport, so I better pay attention and don't get lost. I tried asking more about Garbon, like what it looked like, but she went back to her device, ignoring me.

I hope Garbon is going to be better than this

planet. It's the moon Mer that has this Catalina, that they will imprison me for the time being. I tried asking her how Garbon compares to this place, but she just looked at me keeping to what she was doing. My time with her will not be pleasant. The vibes that come off her I can feel that she doesn't like me, but I'm feeling the same way. Being both females, I assumed we would be more friendly toward each other. Females from other

galaxies, I assume, don't have that friendship. She's more like the violent males I have come across so far. Maybe living here with them for so long makes you become like one. I will never let that happen to me.

The space port was a big change from the area I came from. Much cleaner, but it is still nothing compared to the worst port in Ca'Vais, well, the ones I've seen. People were bustling all around, heading to small shuttle ships. Those ships would take us to the transport ships above the planet's atmosphere. The

small ships flew so close to each other, shockingly not colliding. Tatiana saw my amazement at how they were maneuvering and told me they use autopilot and a routing system to get them out of the atmosphere without crashing. The Laop females were smiling and excited, acting like totally different people from before. This was probably going to be their last time in this

galaxy, and they were happy to be free and leave this despicable place. I have only been here for maybe a day now and I understand them already. Tatiana started telling me it would be wise for me not to give much information to people in this area. They use it to harm you or someone close to you. I don't understand, but

I'm going to follow her advice for right now, since she knows all about that violent stuff. Plus, maybe that was the reason the two Laops wouldn't give me their name. By writing in this book, I guess it makes me look very suspicious. They might think I would sell their names to someone. Wow, I'm going to have to think in these ways now to understand why people will act in a certain way. Nothing is showing good about coming here. I really wanted to know their names and be my true first friends outside my galaxy.

I understood now why she told me to not get lost. There were people all around haggling with others that held red cards in the air. Tatiana would walk to one of

them, talking to them about something I couldn't hear. My primary focus was to dodge all the people walking around, almost running into me, and then focus on her. It didn't take long for Tatiana to find a ship for the other two. The place they were going to seems to be very

popular because most of the ships traveling were going there. The planet was Slytia, on the opposite side of this star system where we are heading, so this was going to be my last time seeing them. There is a Laop embassy that will give them a ticket back to their galaxy. They

wouldn't have to pay anything. I haven't known them for long, but I was going to miss them. Being in such a traumatized situation, I've gained a quick fawn toward them.

It was finally time for them to depart and everyone stood in a circle quiet, not knowing what to say. I opened up by giving them both an enormous hug, while Tatiana made a weird look on her face. She gave a weak hug back to them, not understanding why she was doing this, but didn't want to offend. I think everyone felt it was awkward too but did it anyway just for me. People around also stared like it was a weird action. Back in my galaxy, it was a normal thing to do when a person you see as a friend was leaving, and maybe for the last time. Jasi was still in her mood so did little sitting in a chair, still looking down pathetically.

With the Laop females boarded and off to their destination, it was now time for us to find ours. It didn't take me long to figure out Tatiana wasn't just asking which ship was heading to Garbon; she wanted to find the cheapest price. We have been walking around the place going in complete circles, re-asking some people with the red cards. Some would laugh at her, saying I'm not doing that for that price and for that many

people. Suspicious people started looking over at us. This was getting tiring to the point of stopping and demanding her when she was going to buy the tickets. This seemed to have really irritated her. She said to me, while holding back her anger, she had to find a pleasant trip at a reasonable price because it was killing her pockets bringing along an extra person after paying for two others to go to another planet the opposite way. The pirates were also all in this area and she's having to figure out how to avoid as many as possible.

She finally found us a ship that was going to Garbon. We have one room on the ship and can get some food and drinks; she underlined the drink part. After that, she didn't really talk that much, and dragged us along like children, pulling my hand if I was looking

around for too long. Getting in line, she held my hand and Jasi saying that we really need to watch our surroundings. People were trying to find an opportunity to snatch us up. I wasn't aware until I started looking around at faces. Some were obviously not trying to stare at me. Now looking at everyone, I saw shady people among them not buying tickets but looking around at people. It seemed like they were targeting people. This place looks like a nice place on the outside compared to what I've seemed so far, but everything about this place is disgusting.

Riding up on the short ride to the transport ship

allowed me to see some of the planet's surface, which was exactly what Tatiana described as nothing but dirt and mountains. The transport ship was cleaner than what I have seen in this galaxy, but Tatiana quickly said to me that the Laop galaxy operates this ship, knocking away my thought that Neetoi had something good. The room on the ship was small, and Jasi plotted down in an area I was going to lie down. I said nothing, but I knew she did it on purpose. Her mood was getting on my nerves now. Tatiana set down in her mood also, not

saying much anymore, putting in earpieces, listening to her device. I hope they will be somebody at the bar that I can befriend because I don't want to spend my time with just these two people.

Chapter 14

The long trip to Garbon (Willy)

"Wow! Did you see all that!? That was one of the craziest things I have ever witnessed in my life. I can't believe she could get out of that situation with those pirates. Man! I thought they were going to kill everyone on the train. Hey, can I get another round?" The nervousness and fear still hadn't subsided from me. The only things that help me calm down are drinking and talking. I was shaking from the situation non-stop for the first hour on board. Even though everyone on the train was there too, I couldn't knock the shakes off me. People kept walking up and asking if I was okay, and all I could say was yes. After a couple of drinks, I felt a little calmer. Those women were in a cart further down the train away from me. I know they will get into more

dangerous situations down the road. I don't want to be anywhere near them when those issues happen. Those pirates are going to be after them, and no matter where they go, they will find them. They heavily controlled this area, and they are nothing nice. The bartender handed me another drink, and I downed it in two gulps. "Someone told me you're going to the Sanchi?" A business type looking man said next to me. He looks

very out of place and must be from another galaxy, with the nice clothes he wears, couldn't have gotten that from any place on Gavian. Why is this man starting a conversation with me?

"Yes, love traveling to Mer, well I mean going to that

city. The moon is a total mess right now. Been like that for years, though. Why is a person like yourself in this galaxy? You don't fit the image that you would come to this type of place." The drinks now have me saying everything that was on my mind. These are personal questions I shouldn't be asking, but I'm feeling good and glad to be having a conversation with someone who is not from Gavian.

"I don't think this place is that bad. Some places do not look great, but there are a lot of beautiful places in this galaxy. Have you ever been to Slytia? That place is so beautiful! I'm going back there for business and going to watch a couple of fights at the colosseums. After that, I'm going to head to the Sanchi for a couple of drinks before I leave here." Signaling the bartender for a drink, I was speechless from what he had told me. It was a dream for me to go to Slytia. They do not allow Neetoi

people who do not have the special id cards to get in. Being only told by travelers that it is the most beautiful place in the galaxy, mainly populated by people that are not even from this galaxy. I have known no one being able to get a special id card. What does he do to go watch fights and travel to the other side of the star system to have some drinks? I asked the bartender for another drink again, knowing this was going to be the drink that would drive me over the hill.

"What… How… I want to be life you!" Is all I could say, trying to ask what he did for a living. The drinks had me not thinking and speaking correctly. It was

still going to be awhile before we would get to the spaceport. I can sleep it off. I couldn't afford a separate room, so I was going to have to find a seat and sleep. It's going to be very uncomfortable for me, but I had no other choice. The man could see I had drunk more than

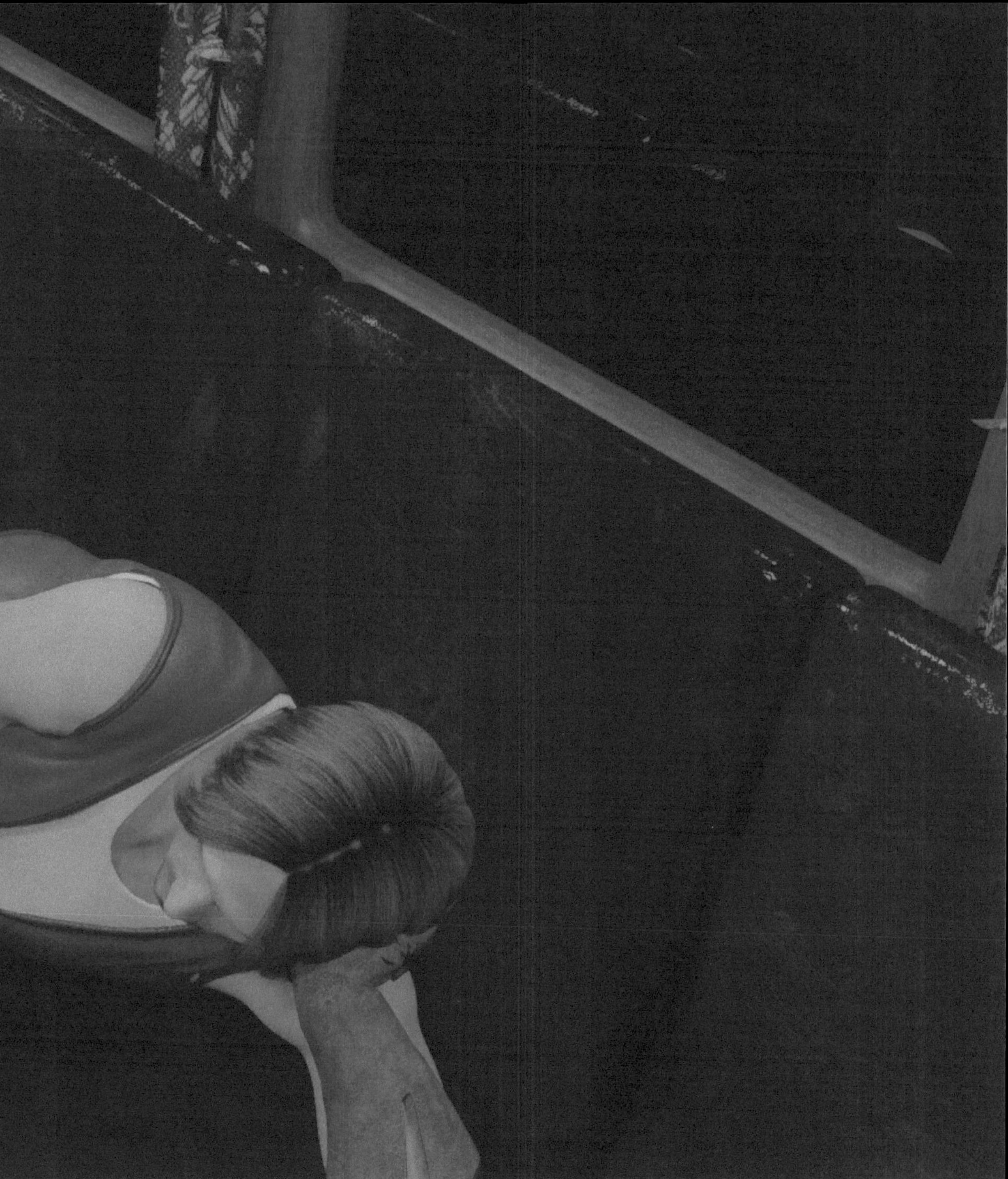

I could handle.

"Hahaha, yup, you have had too much to drink, my friend. You can sleep it off in my room. I have a lot of space, so it won't be a hassle. By the way, you wouldn't want to have my life. My life is filled with boring,

mundane, and pathetic work." My conscious was going in and out and that's what was the last thing I could hear from him before passing out. He picked me up and carried me into his room. I gave a brief fight. Being from Gavian, this wasn't a pleasant situation to be in. This is how someone would kidnap you and have you working in some crazy plant for the rest of your life. My brief fight was nothing for him. He easily knocked off all my defensive attacks like I was playing with him. Having his drink in one hand and holding me in the other. That was the very last thing before I passed out. "Hey! Can you hear me, sir? We're here, sir." An attendant tug on my shirt, waking me up. My eyes opened to see her looking at me with worry. I guess she thought I was dead or something. She kept her hands over her nose, letting me know I wasn't smelling too fresh. Washing up was out of the question for me now. It was going to be a stinky day for me as I began my way to the ship, departing for Garbon. I thanked her, walking out of the room quickly, not giving her enough time to ask for a tip. I knew she was going to be asking for one, for waking me up. The man who let me stay in his room had left. He was very helpful to let me stay

here, to sleep off the drinks. I wonder if I'll run into him again when he goes to the Catalina.

I stepped off the train looking above, seeing all the shuttle ships flying around, dodging each other with ease. On the ships, it doesn't feel like how it looks from being on the ground. I knew they programmed every ship to not bump into each other, but I always am afraid that one day they would fail and cause a colossal disaster. Okay, now it's time for me to find my shuttle ship to my transport ship. Even though this space port is very busy and more organized than anything on this planet, they don't have a wall of information showing you where to find your shuttle ship. Sometimes you must use other shuttle ships just to get in space and get on a space transfer port. I think they do all this to confuse you because if you miss your ship, that's on you. Every brief service here is its own little company, so no one is obligated to get you onto a ship. The key thing that everyone must do here is go through another security line. The Laop military guard this, so there's more seriousness to it. I wonder how… I look back in the line and there are three of the females that caused all the commotion. Some people that were in line knew too, and stayed a few distances away from them, trying not to get caught up in anything that might happen. They shouldn't be able to pass this line since one has a weapon for sure. Now that I think about it, that's Tatiana from the Catalina, and she's a server. I wonder if they are all servers. Well, if they make it to the Catalina, I guess one will serve me.

Passing the security line wasn't a problem for me. There wasn't much to declare or show. Having nothing but my ticket and id card made it go smoothly. The females weren't a care for me, so I didn't look back to see what was going to happen to them. I was now on my way to Garbon, which was a lot better than Gavian. I always search for some type of work when I am there.

If I could be able to live there, it would be a lot better than Gavian. Mer is a very terrible place right now. With the constant wars going on, there is no place safe besides the city walls where the Catalina is. I'm glad I could find my seat with no problems. Luckily, it was still available, and I set down, ready to take another nap. I really wasn't sleepy, but because I smelled, I didn't want to see all the stares I'm getting for being this smelly.

"Damn Willy! Out of all the seats and ships, your seat is next to me. And you stink! Do you know how to wash yourself?!" I open my eyes and look to my side to see Officer Kopolan sitting next to me.

Chapter 15

New Assignment in the Far District

I know they are sending me far off to this crappy
galaxy to get rid of me. Honestly, being the best
operative while being so young, they feel that I'm a
threat. My accomplishments say a lot about my service
and faith in the government. They need to look at

that when they plan my next assignment. They are imbeciles, not giving me any information on what I'm going to be doing here. All they told me was to land here in Gavian and wait for my handler to give me the assignment.

Landing, I could tell there wasn't much to look at here. The maps have many blacked-out areas, preventing the locals from traveling outside areas the military doesn't want them to explore. Even if nothing was blacked out, there wasn't much to look at. They had mysterious places even our military doesn't venture off to, but I have heard nothing special.

The space port was mediocre compared to the ones in the Laop galaxy. I started walking around the food areas, in hopes my handler would spot me, since I didn't know what the person looked like, but they said they could find me.

"Hi, I assume you're Nasia. I'm going to be helping you with your new job out here." An average-looking man approached me. He didn't seem at all military, so I kept walking, thinking that this person wasn't the one I was looking for.

"Okay, you got me. I'm not your actual handler, but they paid me to give you your assignment." He continued walking by my side, "I do a little work here and there for the Laop government, and they told me they will pay me big for giving you this mission. If I do well, I will be your main informer for your handler, and that would mean I get the big money. Sorry for talking about myself. Let me start with your assignment. There is a big organization of pirates that operates out here, called the Deadly Cove Pirates. Your assignment is to get close to them and gather as much information about them and report it back to your handler. You won't be giving that information to me. I guess your people still don't trust us. Here is a ticket to the planet Garbon. There is a bar on the planet Mer where a lot of pirates hang out. That is a great place for you to build your cover and get close to the group." He slid me the paper, which also had another slip in it.

"Your handler also gave me this. Told me it was for you and only you to read. I didn't read it; I know about those letters, and don't want any problems. I want to keep the money coming in, so that's why I'm handing it to you in the same fashion that they handed it to me. That's all I got for you, but to give you some personal information. Those pirates are a very nasty bunch. They have an enormous base here on this planet, but

our government blocks most of the information about it out. They are deep in the trafficking business and have some type of operation going on in Slytia. That bar has all the low lives from all the galaxies around here, so I would be careful if I were you. There is a shuttle ship

that is going to the transport ship that will take you
to Garbon. It's leaving in a few. I will take you there.
Good luck on your mission! The longer you stay alive,
the more chances I have to making more money." He
smiled and showed me the way to the ship. The deadly

Cove Pirates is a group that started in the Laop galaxy but was banished out into this galaxy by the military. I wonder who the leader is now, since most of the ones that started the group are dead or in a Laop prison rotting away. I walked past the security line showing my credentials and left the informer.

I opened the paper that my handler had given the informer. The note read that my assignment was to

infiltrate the group, but also to kill any of them without being noticed. I'm to do anything in my powers for them to trust me and accept me in their group. If I can kill the leader, then I have full permission.

So, the primary aim is to thin out the members by killing them without being suspected. Second, gather as much information about them and relay it to the Laop military. That gave me a sigh of relief. I thought I

was being demoted in intelligence gathering. My main
profession in the Laop is assassination operations, so
I assumed this was a mission punishing me for my
last mistake. I shouldn't have any problems with this
mission, since I know a lot about the pirates that I will
be hunting. I never met a member, but the military has
an extensive record of them.

"Hey someone told me you were military and on
assignment." A Laop soldier walked up to me. Laop
people always look out for each other, which sometimes
becomes a problem, since I'm on assignment and do not
want my cover blown.

"Yes, but I'm on assignment, so it's best not to talk to
me that much." I tried to be nice, since he looked young

and knew little about the rules.

"Sorry about that. I should have known. I just wanted to let you know that we have some pirates on board, and we're keeping a close eye on them. We are searching for one of their members, who is assumed to be their leader. He is in this planetary system, but we haven't found his ship's whereabouts." This was great luck for me. I guess the military is also openly looking for the leader of the group, while I'll be working covertly doing the same.

"Thanks, that's good to know. Can you do me a favor? Don't monitor the pirates on board. I'll monitor them myself and report the information to my superiors. If you find any information about the leader, let me know,

but not around any pirates." He got excited, thinking he was doing something special for the military. He agreed and gave me a salute before marching off.

It wasn't long for me to spot the pirates heading to the transport ship. They didn't seem to hide the fact that they were pirates. Are they able to operate so openly in this area? They are armed but about to pass a Laop security line. There was no issue with them walking through the security line. They were laughing and talking without a care, passing all the military guards who didn't do a thing about them being armed. I see this place is corrupt even within our military, but my primary purpose here is to kill them. They were going to the same ship as me, so I guess they were heading toward Garbon. I guess it's time to start my operation.

Chapter 16

Heading to our quick vacation

"Yo Mikeo! Next time, we should have hijacked a ship to get to the bar. Right?" I hit him on the shoulder, joking with him. People stood around us as we waited in this stupid line. They looked in fear, knowing that we would do it. I looked back, making them turn their heads, not trying to look at me directly. Stupid fools! They should mind their business if they don't want to hear my conversation.

The Laop guard, that was on duty, knew us and let us walk right past, knowing we had our weapons on us. We still had some more time with our so-called vacation from our last job and wanted to head to the Catalina for a couple of drinks before we went back to the major base. The only thing that was fun about this area was the slave chicks we owned. If I didn't let Avian know, I could have my pleasure with all of them. Life was grand now, and we really didn't have any competition or issues.

Mikeo and I walked up to our room, putting some of our stuff down.

"Hey D, let's head to the bar and get some drinks." He said as I put my assault rifle bag down on the seat. That was exactly what I was thinking. We hadn't had a drink in a couple of hours and was needing one right

now. I left the rifle and just kept my side arm, ready for anything. There is Laop military on this ship, but I didn't have any problems with any of them. It shouldn't have to be used, but just in case. Mikeo followed suit. "You think we might have to use these? We gonna have to do some crazy shit to get out of the situation. I'm down if you're down." He smiled, knowing that I didn't

care what would happen, but we would get out of the
situation no matter what. He was my right-hand man, so
I knew he had my back, and I got his.

"Let's go find some chicks for this long ride. Drinks
and ladies are what I'm looking for right now." I said
back to him. He gave a big smile followed by let's go.
We headed for the bar.

After our second drink around the bar scoping the
scene, there wasn't anyone special. We had to leave

because we couldn't bear the smell much longer. A guy
there gave off an awful smell and kept drinking and
talking, trying to start a conversation with anybody that
looked at him. I was going to kick his ass, but Mikeo
stopped me, saying it wasn't worth it. He was down for
me, causing a commotion, but he didn't want to do it
for something so small. We walked around investigating
rooms, seeing if we can rob anyone or steal any bags.

We were making good money robbing the people

in the rooms that we could easily intimidate. The ones that looked like they would fight back we left them alone, not wanting to waste losing chances on the profits we have made by now. If we had to pay off the Laop soldiers, we didn't want to lose all what we have gotten today.

"Hey, isn't that Tatiana the server?" Mikeo was looking

into a room.

"Hello how are you two doing?" A young pretty lady said to us, walking up from behind. I felt a little uneasy because I didn't hear her walking up behind us. Mikeo felt the same way.

"Hey beautiful, what are you doing right now?" Mikeo walked up to her, trying to get a better look at her. By

this time, Tatiana had noticed us at the door. She didn't smile like usual and just stared. Her hand was on her weapon, which seemed very odd. I smiled, opening the door, and walking into the room. Mikeo continued talking to the young lady. As I walked into the room, Mikeo and the lady followed behind. Tatiana didn't like the fact we just barged in, but she knew that there wasn't much she could say about it. She wasn't at the Catalina, so her rules didn't matter on this ship, and she was going to see how we do things outside of her world. She didn't have any problems with me, so it was strange she was acting so uptight. We were heading to the bar and going to spend a lot of this money, so she should be happy and hoping we would tip her nice. The others acted frightened, looking totally terrified like we came to kill them. I felt good that we made a presence like this. One of them seem to look familiar but I couldn't name where I knew her from.

"Hey Tata, how are things going with you and these beautiful ladies?" She hesitated for a second as I held my hand out, waiting for her to shake it. She paused for a couple of seconds while the ladies looked at her, now sweating bullets. Something didn't seem right with them, but she quickly changed her attitude and shook

my hand. By this time, Mikeo had stopped talking to the lady, watching Tata's response, also noticing the weirdness.

"I'm sorry. It's been a rough day for me and now I'm taking back some new employees. Where have you two been? I didn't see you two on Gavian." She normally

didn't come to this area. I guess she saw some of us down there. I think Avian had to pick up some female slaves today.

"Oh no, we weren't on that crappy planet for long. We are having a brief vacation and going to the bar to get some drinks. We came from Slytia watching the fights.

I guess Avian was on Gavian. If I would have known he was there, we could have got a ride with him. We came from the Slytia transport ship and were only at the station on Gavian." I spoke, not enjoying our base on that dirty planet. It doesn't have nothing there. The one who looked familiar kept hiding her face. I was about to say something about it when Tata spoke.

"Hey who is she?" Pointing at the lady that was with Mikeo, I also knew nothing about her. Why did she follow us into the room?

Chapter 17

Uncomfortable Situation

This was now becoming a terrible situation. I messed up when they barged into the room, thinking that I had locked the door. Big mistake. These were two very violent and insane members of the Deadly Cove Pirates. I never thought I would run into them on this ship. The only positive thing going for us is they don't know what happened on Gavian. They don't seem to recognize Jasi either, so it might go well if I can get them out of the room, quickly.

That female they brought in is some sort of soldier. I'm thinking that she's Laop, but she hasn't identified herself. She's probably here investigating something or someone. After asking who she was, I could see Dwayne was thinking the same thing. I guess he didn't know who she was. Even though these two are very wild and violent, they are not dumb, and will notice anything out of place. Mikeo knows Jasi is trying to hide her face from them, but is giving me some respect. I shouldn't worry about anything, but only if he knew. Luckily, Jasi and Viviana caught on, so they're doing the best thing by keeping their mouths shut. They looked like ghost when they barged in. If I hadn't started talking, I think they would have tried to make a run for the door.

"I'm sorry, everyone, for just barging in with these two. I'm a dancer from Slytia and was passing them and just sparked up a conversation. I don't have anyone in my room, so was bored and wanted some people to chat with." She was obviously lying, but they seemed to accept it for now. I didn't want any of them in the room but couldn't just outright say it, making them suspect I was hiding something. The room fell silent. I didn't know if they were thinking about what she said, or about why I was acting so strange. At the bar, they know me as a delightful conversationalist, but today I had nothing to say. I still had my gun out, which made them feel uneasy.

"I wish I could have seen you dancing when I was there on Slytia." Mikeo said. Suddenly, their radios chirped. Dwayne picked up his, while Mikeo went into a deep thought. Mikeo wasn't saying anything while Dwayne listened to the person on the other end. I didn't have a good feeling about who he was talking to, but kept my composure, relaxed sitting back, not trying to alarm anyone in the room. Keeping my eyes on the two, I couldn't see how Viviana and Jasi were doing. Things didn't look like they were going to go well. Dwayne listened, shaking his head, and finally said,

"Understood!" at the end of his conversation. He put up his device and stared down at the floor.

At this moment, the mood in the room changed. He opened his eyes, looking me in the eye. I knew it was Avian on the other line. Dwayne now knows. I wasn't looking at some customer from the bar anymore; I was looking at an enemy. He was about to say something when Mikeo spoke first. "You weren't on the transport ship. There were many people, but I can say for a fact that you weren't on that ship. You didn't come with us from Slytia!" Mikeo angrily said, standing up in front of her. A soldier suddenly walked into the room, looked directly at the dancer. My eyes stayed

locked with Dwayne's. He didn't care either about the commotion. He was looking at someone he needed to kill. I had my weapon out, while he didn't have his out. I didn't think I could shoot him successfully and kill Mikeo without Jasi or Viviana dying. Also, I didn't know how the other two in the room would respond. Are they working with the pirates?

The soldier stood in the middle of the door, dumbfounded, not knowing what to do. Mikeo went for his weapon, not taking any chances, aiming it at the lady. That caused the soldier to reach for his weapon, making Dwayne break eye contact with me, rolling on the floor, and pulling his weapon out in the motion. He

finished his roll, shooting two shots into the soldier's chest, killing him. Viviana and Jasi cowered in the corner. Mikeo wrestled with the young female who went for the gun. The lady didn't have enough strength to overpower him and wasn't able to get the weapon out of his hand, but he couldn't aim to shoot her. She pulled out a blade, almost slicing his wrist, causing him to drop the weapon. Automatically grabbing it, she took a couple shots at Dwayne; him luckily escaping unscathed out of the door. Mikeo flashed some type of device, blinding everyone in the room, making her unable to get a shot off, as he ran out of the room

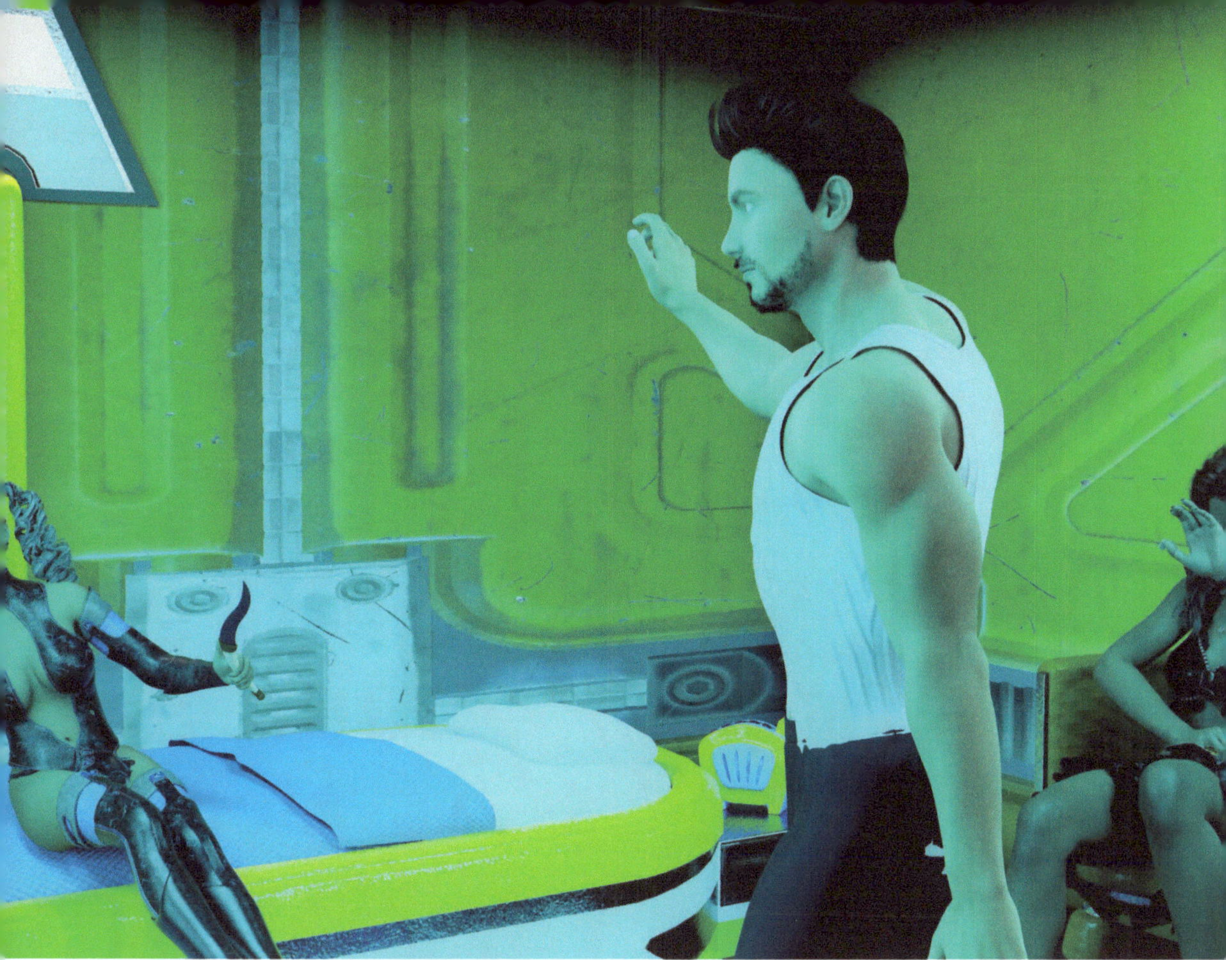

behind Dwayne. The female, with no hesitation and concern for us, chased after them.

Jasi and Viviana were still in shock as the unwanted guest finally cleared the room. Well, not almost. There was a dead body that was in-between the door. I guess I will have to slide it outside the doorway for it to close. We have a long way to get there and with just this handgun and two crazy pirates running around this ship; I don't know if this is going to be enough. At least the military is after them now.

"I guess we're going to be seeing a lot of this. On our way to the bar." Sitting back in my seat after sliding the

body outside of the room. Wonder who that female was and why she lied. She seems to be after them, hence why she said nothing to us as she ran out of the room. That would be terrible problems, the Laop military after me, and these stupid pirates. Pops is going to pay me big for this!

Chapter 18

Some Vacation

DECK
6

LANG

"So, what's the plan D?" I said to him, looking back to see if the female was following us. She had my weapon and probably had more hidden. She must be military, but why did she lie? Were they after us?

"Right now, we need to find somewhere to hide. They are definitely going to be looking for us for murdering that soldier. Avian was on the radio and told me what happened on Gavian." The lady suddenly appeared from behind, shooting. Luckily, we were turning a corner, so she couldn't hit us, but if we weren't quick enough, she would have shot me in the head. She wasn't a normal soldier with those types of skills. This is serious. Not having a weapon made me at a tremendous disadvantage. D shot back, trying to keep her at bay. I took the lead, trying to figure out how to get out of this mess. The ship is enormous with about four levels. We could easily find a room to hide in, but first we had to lose her. If we can get back to our rooms, we can get our rifles and take over the bridge. I knew Avian's ship was somewhere in the area, giving us an escape.

We kept running down hallways one after another, bumping into people. The lady kept chasing, ignoring the passengers. I thought they would give a brief

distraction to her, but to no avail. We hadn't run into any soldiers, but that was a bad sign, meaning they were setting up an area to trap us. Most ships like this would have about two hundred soldiers on board, but with many small confinements, their numbers won't be a problem. But if they catch us in an open space, we are done.

Turning a corner, I had to jump back just in time to dodge a burst of rounds hitting the wall. There were a couple of soldiers around the corner pinning us. We couldn't go back because now the female had two extra

soldiers helping her with the chase.

"This doesn't look good, D." I said with my hands out, reminding him I didn't have a weapon. He looked over, tossing the weapon into my hand, "You the idiot that got his weapon taken. Here, you deal with this situation if you can't think of a way to get out of this mess. Let the real brain get into action." I started shooting at the female group, keeping her at bay for the time being while randomly shooting back at the soldiers around the opposite corner. That prevented them from advancing, but I knew none of my shots would hit any of them.

By this time, the doors were all locked. We couldn't open doors like we had been doing. D went

over pulling out his hacking device and started working
on a door, trying to get it open.

From having to shoot the gun so much, it was
overheating and shooting slower. This allowed the
soldiers around the corner to move closer and closer.
We had little time before it was going to be a big
problem for us. I wasn't getting the impression that they
wanted to take prisoners. I looked over at D, who was
working at it. The door finally opened, and we rushed
in, while it closed right behind us.

We had some time to think now. They weren't
going to be able to open that door for a while. When
they locked all the doors, it takes a while for them

to unlock. On these types of ships, they must unlock all the doors to just unlock this one. If they do that, it will allow us to use the elevators and everything to find more places to hide. They could keep the doors locked until a battleship or more soldiers were here, able to capture us without an incident. No matter which decision they choose, it's going to be a problem for us if we don't figure out how to get off this ship.

"Okay, we have some time to think. That weapon is going to have to rest for a while before we can shoot it. This is horrible, only having one weapon and all these soldiers after us." I said, while D was already working on a plan.

"We should be able to get out of this. This is just another regular day, compared to the things we get into all the time. You saw how Tatiana was acting funny around us earlier? Well, the females that she had with her are our property and she stole them from Avian. He told me to capture them and Tatiana. If she doesn't come with us, then we are to kill her." I looked at him now, remembering that I saw one of those females around Avian before. This was a shock for Tatiana's character. I didn't see her as a thief, but in this galaxy, you never know who is.

"Should we try to get them first and then take over the ship?" I said, ready to get our property back.

"Right now, we need to get some rifles because we won't be able to fight the military with just a gun. If we could somehow get back to our rooms, then we would be better off." When D said that we heard a loud bang on the door, they were trying to get in. I guess they would not unlock the doors and decided just to break down this door. This ship used to be military, so it was going to take them sometime to break down the doors. What they didn't know, which I just remembered, is that they did not protect the walls as much as the doors. I looked over at D, who seemed to remember also about the walls, taking apart devices in the room to make a mini explosive. I guess our vacation is over.

Chapter 19

Hope I get an assist

I can't believe he was stupid enough to just walk into the room. Didn't I tell him not to contact me if I was around pirates? Now the two were trapped in a room. Who contacted him on his radio and what did they say? Was that their leader telling them we were on them? Why did he get really serious after that call? I can't have these two jeopardizing my operation this soon. They are going to have to die here to better my chances of infiltrating the group. Who were those females that they seem to know? They didn't seem like pirates, but one had a weapon and didn't mind showing it. I thought they banned weapons, but I have already seen a couple, and one has killed my kind. They are going to pay for that.

"The commander of the ship says that he will not unlock the doors for security reasons." A soldier said to me as we tried to get through the door. What was he thinking? I needed to interrogate and kill them before arriving on the planet. Knowing I couldn't communicate this over the radio and not being able to leave this area was a challenge for me. They only have a weapon, so they know we out gun them. What are they going to do? This was not starting off good for me. I nodded to the soldier, knowing that I couldn't say

R-0566
R-0586
0586
TECH LAB

anything to change his mind. It would just get him into trouble.

"Get me information on the nearest battleship to this ship." I tried telling the soldier, but another grabbed him, stopping him from doing what I had told him. "Who are you?" The person approached me. I was guessing he was the commander of all the soldiers here. "I'm with the Laop military and on a secret mission." He stopped me. "If you are on a secret mission, then this doesn't pertain to you. I run all operations here on this ship and this situation is for me to manage. If you are on a secret mission, shouldn't you be undercover acting like a regular passenger instead of commanding a fire team to kill pirates?" He waved off a couple of soldiers dwindling down the numbers at the door. "I need to interrogate those two before we get to the planet." He cut me off again. "Look, that is your problem. I can't help you. Right now, my mission is to capture or kill these pirates who have murdered one of my soldiers. I am dismissing you from this area and someone will escort you to your room. You are to remain in your room until we make it to the planet and from there you can get off my ship and do whatever you like."

"You know we work for the same military, right?" I said, shocked that instead of us working together, he was confining me into my room.

"Look, we deal with pirates all the time here in this galaxy. Just because you are coming here on your little special assignment doesn't mean you can come around and act wild and do whatever you like. From you being

here, I have a dead soldier. I don't have time talking
to you anymore. I will get two soldiers to escort you
back to your room." He didn't wait for my answer and
walked off to the door, telling them to stop damaging
the door. I knew it would just cause more problems for
me if I tried arguing with him, so I just gave up and
followed the soldiers back to my room.

Heading back to the room, I thought about it some more and realized that him killing them was going to be a suitable solution. Putting in the report that I killed them would have been great, but I should be able to get an assist. I hope the stupid commander writes nothing

about the death of the soldier being my fault, since it wasn't technically my fault, anyway. He should have known better and listened to what I had told him.

It was going to take around two days to get to the planet, so that would give me plenty of time to rest and

get focused. One pirate mentioned the female worked at a bar. I wonder if he was talking about that bar I was told about. Why would a bartender have a weapon? I shouldn't have followed them and instead stayed in that room to get to know them better. Now being confined to my room, I won't be able to talk to them.

The locks were still in place, making us walk up long emergency elevators, taking some time for us to get there. If we kept at it trying to destroy the door, we should have been in there by now and the situation would have been over. We were too far to hear anything now so didn't know what was going on, but they had stopped. Once we got to the floor, we walked into a mass group of people that were outside waiting to get back inside their room since they were outside when all the things happened.

Guess I will wait out here like them, I thought. As soon as I approached my door, all the locks unlocked. The soldiers followed behind me as I walked into my room. My guess was that they were going to check inside and stand guard by the door. I didn't care anymore and was going to get in the bed and just rest the rest of the trip. Laying on my bed, I closed my eyes, falling into a deep sleep, but the last thought that crossed my mind was with the doors. Being that they were now unlocked, the pirates had access to the command cockpit. They wouldn't be that dumb enough to hijack this ship. Right?

Chapter 20

Vacation Over

If everything plays right, then we will get some
weapons and get out of this situation somehow.
Well, not out of the whole situation, but we will have
weapons and will fight. We took cover in the back
of the room, away from where I had placed a small
explosive. The blast should be strong enough to make
a hole. The soldiers' that guard transport ships had the
procedure of killing us pirates as quickly as possible, so
they were going to unlock the doors, eventually. They
are confident in their soldiers, so I knew their strategy
was to come in from the front, knowing that we only

had one weapon. I looked over at Mikeo, nodding to him to get ready.

The doors finally unlocked, and I detonated the device, blasting debris everywhere. I'm happy I used the right amount that didn't blow the outside frame, sucking us out into space. We jumped through the hole that it made and ran as fast as we could, turning toward the door. Mikeo had the lead because he had the weapon and as soon as we opened the door, we saw their tactical team enter the room they assumed we were still in as the secondary team stood guard, not expecting

us to come out of the room next door. There weren't
that many outside, so this was going to be easy. Mikeo
shot two in the head, killing them instantly. I grabbed
one of their rifles before they hit the ground as Mikeo
smashed the bud of his weapon on the nose of the third
soldier. They didn't seem like much of a fight because
they were still in shock at what had just happened. This
allowed me to gun down all the ones in the hallway,
including their leader.

The tactical team had avoided us because they had
made it in the room, but I grabbed an explosive that was

on one soldier's belt, throwing it into the room, blasting the room fairly well. We didn't stay to check to see if we killed them and made our escape down the hallway toward some stairs. Should we go after Tatiana's group first or get our things? Sadly, we had to abandon most of our treasure from the passengers. If we take command of this ship, then we can easily get to Tatiana. "Mikeo, we're going to have to get back to our room and get our weapons. If we take over this ship, then we can get to Tatiana anytime." Mikeo stopped me. "I don't think that's a clever idea. Well, I do, but I think we need to get to Tatiana first and then get off this ship. I don't think we need to let her sit while we are doing this. I always had a feeling about her." He was right, since we would cause a lot of commotion and she wasn't going to just sit still. Those other two should slow her down, seeing that they were frightened with everything happening.

"You're right. Let's split up. You grab Tatiana while I get our things and we meet up on the maintenance floor." That place would be a good place to stash our things, since no one traverses there as much.

"Alright." He took off down the hallway toward their area. I headed back to our room. We weren't that far

away. After causing so much violence meant they will sound the alarms again. As I thought about it, the lights began flashing red. I'm guessing someone had survived, or they had found the bodies in the hall. It's time to have some fun, I guess.

Walking in, I could automatically tell that someone had been in the room. Our weapons weren't there. As I turned to walk out, three soldiers entered the room with weapons drawn. Being careless, I didn't set up any traps or had my weapon out. I didn't think they would have come to the room so quickly. I raised my hands, feeling stupid that I had made that mistake, and started

walking toward them. None of them told me to stop, and I noticed they were shaking a little, holding the weapon on me. I smiled and kept walking closer. By the time I got to the muzzle of the weapon, one of them said stop, but it was too late. Stepping close enough to bump our chests together, I head butted him in the nose. He fell to the ground, allowing me to grab his weapon. Taking a step back toward another soldier, now becoming parallel to his weapon, he couldn't turn it on me. I easily knocked his weapon to the floor. The third had his weapon on me the whole time but never shot. I'm guessing he hadn't shot anyone before. He should have shot me because once I push the second one onto the ground, I pulled the trigger on the rifle, shooting him dead in the head.

The other two stayed on the ground, mortified, looking at their dead friend. I kicked the first one in the head, knocking him out while pointing my weapon at the second guy.

"There was some stuff in this room. Where is it?" I said, ready to pull the trigger.

"Wait, wait, wait!!! It's in the security room! I'll take you there! Please don't kill me!" He started wailing in tears. If all these soldiers are going to act like this, then we are going to be okay. I grabbed him by his arm, searching him for any weapons or communication devices, stripping him down to his underwear. Putting his hands above his head, I strapped on two rifles and had my handgun on his back while we walked down the hallway. I made random glances back just to check if anyone was following us. The soldier kept whimpering as we walked.

Looking into the security room, I could see four soldiers. They had their weapons already pointed at the door. They knew I was coming since they were watching me on the security cameras. None of the

soldiers looked like they were leaders. This was good, since it meant most of the leaders were running scared. "Look, if you throw my weapons out here, I won't try to enter. If you let us wait peacefully for our friends to come pick us up, then there won't be any problems. I don't want to kill this man out here, but if you push me, I will do it." I pushed him to the door. They could see his face when I slid the door open. I raised my weapon through the opening, showing them I could easily kill them. Only on the old ships I'm able to unlock them, but the newer models I wouldn't have been able to do any of this. I could only open these doors halfway since they were old ships, but the newer models I wouldn't have been able to. I gave them a chance by not just opening fire on them, since I was guessing they didn't want a fight. They easily surrendered with no fight. I could have killed them, but decided to just tie them up in the room. Now we had a good amount of weapons. I headed my way to the stairs toward the maintenance level.

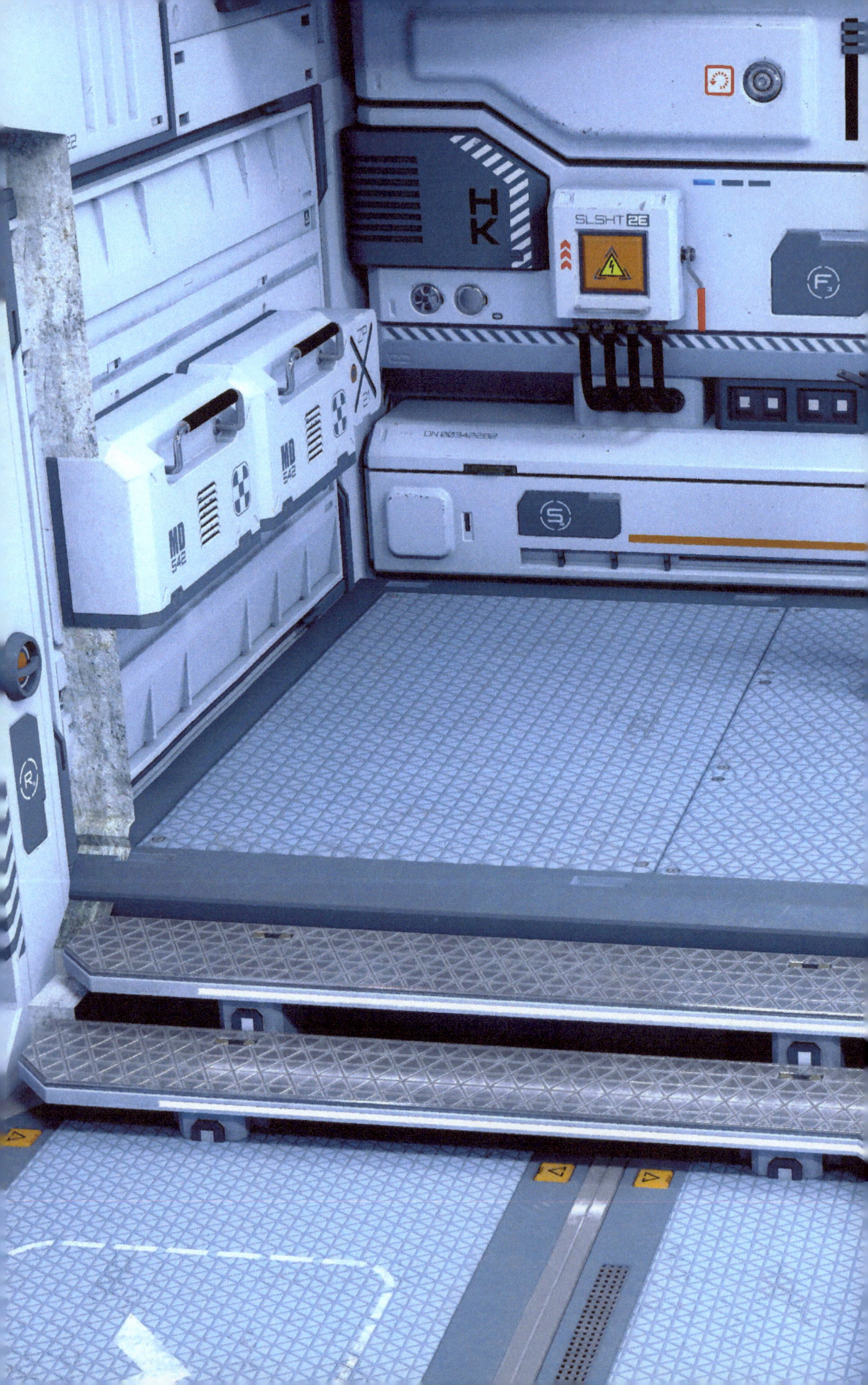

RDS 12
PST 56
SOLARIS F23
DN 00B452231
DN 00B452232
DN 003422B2

Chapter 21

Would Pops forgive me?

Jasi and Viviana were distraught after the ordeal. The blood from the soldier was still fresh and you could smell it. They huddled in the corner, so I picked them up and put them on the bed. The doors locked, which I knew was protocol. Knowing those two, they were going to get out of this mess, but would definitely come looking for us once they got better weapons. We were going to have little time once the doors unlock, and we had to get to another room before they came back here. The only options they had were escaping off this ship or hijack it. Both options meant I would run into Avian before getting to the planet. Damn, are these two bad luck?

I sat thinking of a way to get out of this mess as Viviana just stared at me with some type of confused look.

"What's your problem?" I eventually had to ask. She has been so annoying this whole time.

"How can you live like this?" she said, annoying me more, thinking this is an everyday thing for me. I wanted to tell her it was you two that got me in this mess, and I could end it right now by just turning them over to these pirates. Damn Pops, if it were someone else, I would have quickly killed these two and found

another way to get home. I ignored her question and her stupid stares while trying to think of a place to go once the doors unlocked. That suspicious female I hope won't be a problem while on this ship. I had one weapon, and the one that dropped on the floor. They were going to have some type of heavy weapons by the time these doors were open, so this would not be enough. These two were also going to slow me down.

The best place we could go with no one coming around was the maintenance level on this ship. With those two getting into a firefight, they will probably head to the cockpit or communications room, giving us enough time to find a place on that level to hide until we get to the planet. I didn't think it was going to be a wise idea to tell the others about the plan. It would shake them up pretty badly, so I decided it was the best option. I wonder if I'm going to like these two once they get to the Catalina. Melinda is probably going to kill one of them, but it won't matter after that because Pops would have already paid me.

The doors eventually unlocked, followed by a loud explosion that rocked the ship. I knew that had to

be those two and we were going to have to be quick now. I looked at them. "Alright we need to go. They are probably coming back here right now." As I turned for the door, both stayed sitting down.

"How do you know that? Why would they come back? Soldiers are after them. The best thing we can do is just let the military handle this while we stay in our rooms." Viviana said, trying to take a leadership role.

"She has a point. You just want to go around killing more people. You're just like them! They were just your friends, and you knew they were a bunch of killers, and

so are you." Jasi chimed in.

At that moment, I really thought about my friendship with Pops. He has been looking out for me for a while and pays me pretty well. I have acted in the wrong plenty of times in the past and he has always accepted me back. I wonder if I kill these two right here and just say the pirates did it. Will he believe me? As I was contemplating about killing them, I guess the look on my face told the story and they quickly changed their decisions on staying in the room.

"Maybe you are right. I'm going to follow what you say

because you are the one taking me to the Catalina." Jasi said with Viviana nodding. That was quite easy. This stall cost us a good amount of time. We finally started our move when Mikeo pivoted the corner as I stepped

out, causing me to fire on him. He saw me in time to jump back. I saw he armed himself with a weapon. I looked back at the two, who were both shocked. "I see one. I'm going to shoot down the hallway

to pin him down. You two make a run down the hallway toward the elevator." That's all I could say before I had to react, kicking an explosive out of the room before it exploded. The explosion knocked me back into the room. I didn't let go of my gun, from experience, knowing to just shoot a couple of shots toward the doorway. That saved my life because Mikeo was already making his move into the room, having to roll away from my shots. If I shot a little lower, I would have been able to hit him. I dove toward the wall, rolling onto the bed, dodging the shots from his

132

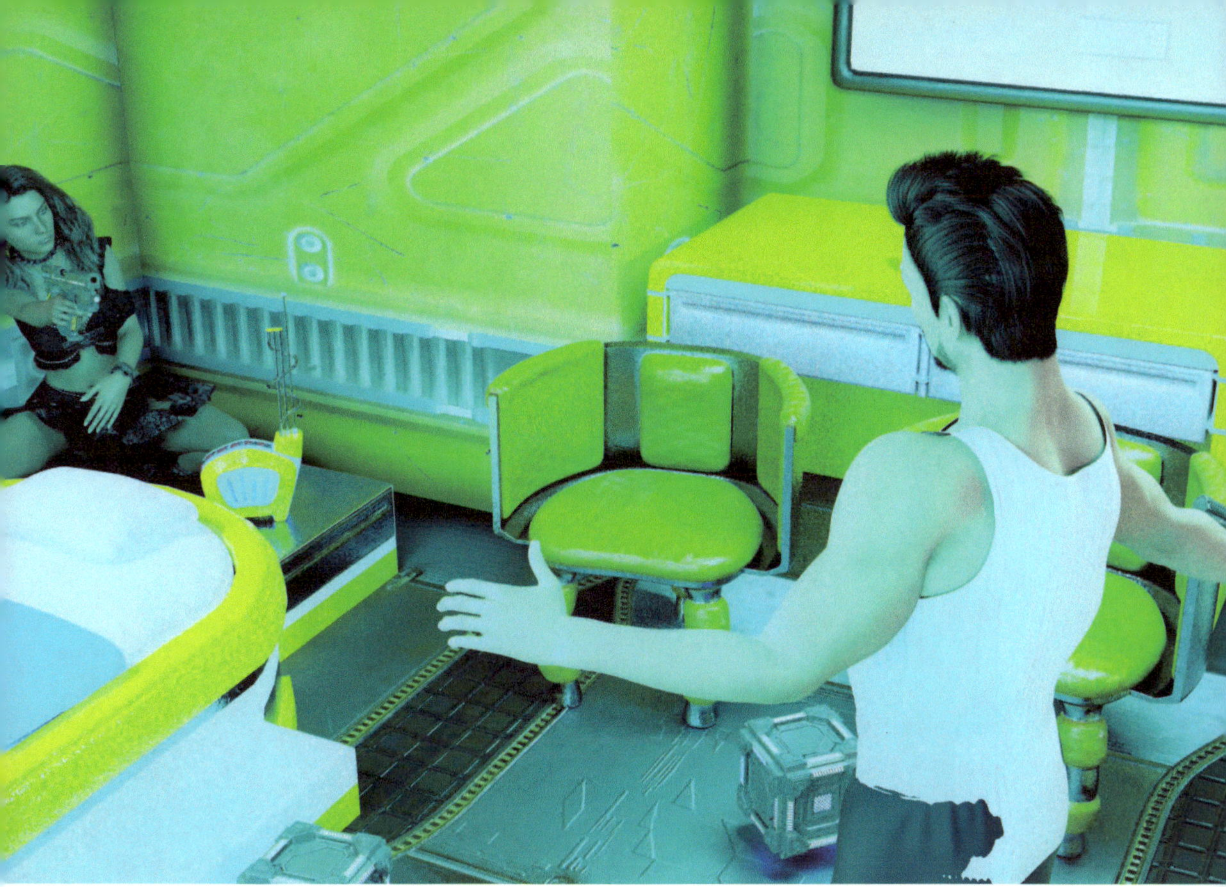

weapon. Everything went quiet until he spoke, not concealed but having a gun on the two.

"You're really cool, Tatiana, and I don't want to kill you, but I'm under orders. These two are coming back because they are ours. If you want to live, I suggest you become a property of ours. You will be treated right." He smiled, walking closer to the two who were cowering back in their corner. I knew we should have run before he got back. It looks like it's just Mikeo, though. He was almost close to them to grab when two soldiers walked into the room and automatically began firing at him, not really caring about the two females. They didn't aim well, not hitting anyone, but giving

me enough time to shoot toward Mikeo, causing him
to jump over behind the other bed. He was still able to
keep his handgun. The soldiers started shooting at me,
causing me to duck down behind the bed. I guess they
don't care who they kill right now. They weren't that
well trained and were standing in the doorway being
perfect targets for Mikeo, who shot them down quickly.
He had to make a run out of the room, knowing that
I had the advantage. I grabbed the two that were still
cowering in the corner and told them we had to leave
now, or he would be back.

Vivi's
Journal

Chapter 22

Where are they?

Please hurry and make it back, Tatiana. I don't know if I can last with you being gone for this long. Thankfully Trish has finally shown up, but she isn't much of a help. She doesn't know how to make drinks and she always forgets who ordered what. I have to walk behind her just to make sure one of these bad customers won't lie and get free food and drinks. The regular customers are always happy to see her working. They should be here by tomorrow, so I should have just one more day of this crap. The customers are getting very annoyed at just seeing me. They can only take glances at Melinda, not wanting to get the evil stare down from her. She doesn't even have to raise her voice to get everyone to fear her. I wish I could do that, but no one fears my regular Neetoi behind. This galaxy is all I know, and I can just repeat stories I have heard about places I want to travel to. But it's nice working here. Thanks to Pops, I get to see many people from all over the universe. Thinking about Pops, where is he? I wish he came down here and helped occasionally. I know he knows that this place is short staff and avoiding this place just to make my life miserable.

While in my deep thought, I heard a glass break from behind. I didn't turn around knowing that it was

just Trish breaking another glass while she tried to wash the dishes. I'm thinking that it's the fifth one she has broken now. Melinda is cracking up from watching her do it, not caring that this was coming out of our paychecks combined.

"Sir! How long are you going to take making my food?!" an angry customer said to me. He was new around here, so I wasn't rude back to him. I was also finishing up his food, so was heading his way to drop it off, anyway. He took the food, giving me a mean stare, tossing some money at me. Looking at his outfit, I

忍者

could tell he was a Mer soldier. I'm guessing he wasn't having such a good day. Turning and heading back to the stove, I heard a loud group come through the door. Trisha, by this time, had finished trying to wash the dishes and grabbed a stool to sit next to me while I cooked. I don't know why she would do this, acting like

she was learning how to cook, but I didn't care. I wasn't going to turn down a beautiful lady sitting next to me. "Give us some beer and some food! We have had a momentous day today!" One person said from the loud group, sitting down at a booth. They seemed new to the city, walking around like they owned the place.

Tatiana was the best in situations like this. With her not around today, I was going to have to be the one to keep everything cool. I nodded at the group, showing that I got their order. Some other customers got angry since they had been waiting longer. Trisha noticed this and walked over, trying to take their order. Melinda looked over at me and nodded. She went back to reading with a smirk. She was laughing at me on the inside, but I couldn't do anything about it. I put five burgers on the stove and prepared the beers. One person from the group walked up to the counter. He was between Melinda and the Mer soldier.

"So, what type of females come to this city?" He said to me. I handed him the beer I was preparing. He wanted to get Melinda's attention, but she kept reading her book.

"I just work all the time here. I see a suitable number of females come here, but I'm always working. So have little time to get involved with any of them." That was the truth, but also the problem with this area is that there are so many spies in this city you can't really trust anyone. Having a relationship with someone and not knowing who they aligned with can get you quickly killed around here. He must not be from this area to ask

a question like this.

"You need to keep your stinking hands off anybody on this planet, Garbage!" The Mer soldier stood up to face the man. When the soldier said Garbage, I realized the man was from Garbon and was probably some type of mercenary sent here to support the Garbon Union. The man's group now stood up and was making their way to the counter. Trouble looked like it was about to start. Before I could say anything about the rules around this place, Melinda closed her book. Oddly, from her closing her book, the vibration shook the whole place

145

quiet. She was still staring down when she spoke. "The Vatician government protects this city. It has been around long before both of your people came to this galaxy. There is a strict rule of no fighting or violence inside these city walls. You all were told this by the guards upon entering the city gates. Looking at the guards makes it seem okay to break the rules. But understand if you choose to break those rules Vaticians will hunt you down no matter where you hide. I suggest you think twice about bickering and bringing your problems within these city walls. Unless you are willing to face the wrath of the Vaticians." She then stood up, never once looking at the group, walking behind the counter and sitting on Trish's stool looking at the food I realized was now burning up. I ran over to flip the burgers. The Mer soldier said nothing while the group went back to their seats, taking glances back at the Mer but not doing anything. I was glad that Melinda was there to have my back and looked at her, giving her a thank you smile. She looked back in disgust, wondering why I did that.

"Idiot. I had to say something to get from around them. Having too many stinking males around was giving me a headache. Also, I'm hungry and I can't have you being bloody while you make my food." That's Melinda for you.

Chapter 23

Major Trouble

Dammit! I can't believe she got the best of me. I should have just grabbed the two females and kept shooting to pin her down. After I secured those two, I didn't have to worry about catching her until later. I didn't know she was that tough. She will be a high-quality product of ours if we can tame her.

Not wasting any more time, I hurried to the stairs to head toward the maintenance level. I stopped realizing that I should go to the cockpit first and secure it. They should all be fearing us by now, seeing we just killed their commander. Getting control of the ship shouldn't be a problem. Then it will be a lot easier to catch Tatiana and the females.

The hallways were empty. I'm guessing no one wanted to be stuck outside again if they locked the doors. That was a good idea because the alarms seemed to go on again. I'm guessing they know about us and searching. Oddly, no one has come out yet and confronted me. Of course, with my dumb luck, three soldiers were prone, waiting for me around the corner. I dove out of their line of fire, rolling and making a run down the hallway. The soldiers were guarding the path that led to the cockpit. They had body armor and rifles, so I wasn't going to be a match for them.

Expecting there would be more soldiers around the next corner, I shot a couple of rounds ahead as I turned the corner. I was right, a soldier was in my path dodging the rounds I had shot. He could return fire but at an angle, missing me. That gave me enough time to shoot enough rounds in the soldier's direction. This allowed me to make it to another hallway. It wasn't just one soldier; I realized as I ran down the hallway. They didn't seem like the basic soldiers assigned to this

ship. I couldn't head back toward the maintenance level the way I came. I know there should be more stairs somewhere.

At the end of the hallway, I saw some stairs, but two soldiers stood guarding it. Luckily, they weren't expecting me, so they didn't have their weapons drawn. If they had been ready for me, I wouldn't be alive. I didn't stop running, heading directly toward them shooting. Both dodged, not being able to shoot back.

ATCH YOUR HEAD

LEVEL
ON

This allowed me to make it to the stairs. When they could shoot back, they hit the stairs in front of me. Dodging the rounds running down the steps, I made it into a door which led to a long hallway. I ran down the hallway, eventually choosing a random door. This led to some type of laundry area. They were following me, but I seemed to have lost them for the time being. They were well-trained soldiers, so I wasn't going to let my guard down. I got to get to Dwayne and tell him about them. He doesn't need to go die trying to attack the cockpit.

From this area, I didn't have a clue where the stairs were to the maintenance level. It would be suicide to get on the elevators, so I stayed hidden inside a big bin with clothes on top. Trying to think of a way out of this mess, two soldiers walked up to the bin, while another ran up to them. I could hear them but couldn't see being under the clothes. I was trying my best not to be heard breathing.

"Did you find them yet?" The one who ran up being out of breath spoke first.

"No, we lost one around this area. It was just one. I don't think the other was with him. I think the last of the reports said it was two pirates held up in a room.

They are Deadly Cove pirates, so we can kill them. We are not taking them prisoner." Another said.

"The only way they can get out of this mess is to hijack the ship or get one of their buddies to come with another ship. That plan will fail once we get near Garbon. We have a couple of ships blockading the area, so no pirate ship will land on the planet. Communications are being jammed now, so they won't be able to contact their buddies on their communication devices."

"We still have to watch out because they have plenty of spies in our military. Once we make the attack on their primary base, they will quickly lose those spies. It will force them to run to another galaxy like how they did back home."

"You two shut up and hurry back. Our mission right now is just to keep the cockpit guarded until we make it to the planet."

They walked off, not noticing me at all. If what they say about attacking the primary base is true, then this is going to be major trouble. They shouldn't know where our primary base is located. The only way they would know is if we had a traitor amongst us, but that is impossible. No matter what, I must get this information to Avian. We must stay away from Garbon since all the Laop ships in the area will be hunting us. I wonder what made them change their view on us in this area. There must be something big about to happen for the Laop military to start operations on us in the Neetoi galaxy.

I jumped out of the bin, walking in the opposite direction the soldiers went. I eventually found some stairs that led me to the maintenance area. The area was quiet of people, but the machinery noise was very loud. I searched for a good place to hide, thinking about what I just heard waiting for Dwayne to show up.

Chapter 24

Salvage my mission

I jumped out of the bed, hearing an explosion going off. I wasn't dead, so it wasn't in this area. My next thought it had to be the pirates, and something had happened. Running toward the door, I stopped, knowing that I would probably get in more trouble if I headed toward the area. I turned back and set in a chair contemplating on what I should do. The commander told me not to get involved and I should let them do their job. They should easily be able to kill two measly pirates. I should put more confidence in my military. I don't have to do everything by myself.

Sitting there, I heard a lot of shooting. The shooting eventually stopped, but I didn't have a good feeling the military had everything under control. I feel the pirates have got the best of them and they are now running around the ship. I knew it wasn't good for me to just sit here. If those two get back to the pirates, I won't be able to infiltrate the group. I can't fail my mission before it even starts.

I opened the door expecting to see the soldiers, but they seemed to have left the door. I guess they went back to see what was going on when they heard the explosion. There was no one outside in the hallways, and it was eerily quiet. I could hear myself walking

down the hallway. I hated I had this outfit on that was a disguise of a dancer from Slytia. None of the soldiers said anything, but I knew they were giving sly glances at me under those goggles. I paid it no mind, though.

I was closer to the room of the females; I headed there instead of the room where the pirates were. Looking at the doorway to the room, it looked like another explosion had gone off. An explosive had ripped up the body of the dead soldier. That made me fill up with anger how they disrespected one of my kind even more. I saw two more soldiers dead between the doors and the females were gone. They must know something about the pirates for them to come back here. Who are they?

I headed back to the room the pirates locked themselves in. I now had my weapon out, ready for anything. Coming onto the scene was like looking at a war zone. The bodies of the soldiers lay out on the floor. The commander was killed too. Looking in the room they were in, I saw they had used an explosive to blow through the wall next door. I'm guessing to escape. There were no bodies, so they had to be alive. I didn't expect two pirates would be this difficult to kill, but time was running out and we were getting closer to the planet. This was giving them more opportunities to escape.

Seeing that they had gone back to the females' room meant they were somewhat important. My main goal was finding them and that will lead me to the pirates. Another option these pirates can do is try to get to the cockpit to get control of the ship. They could also try to go to the communications room and contact their friends, but I doubt they will try that. They also could hide, but that would give the soldiers on the ship enough time to capture them once we get to the planet.

There was too much to think about, but the first thing I had to do was figure out who was in control of this ship now that the commander was dead. I headed to the cockpit.

Almost getting there, I heard a big shootout, so I hid, not knowing what was going on. It eventually subsided, and I headed toward the cockpit.

"Who are you?! Put your hands up!" A soldier said to me while two others were prone to shoot.

"Sorry, I'm with the Laop military on a secret assignment. Who is in charge here?" I said, not having any identification to prove anything. I knew I was going to have some problems.

"Okay, you were in the commander's reports before they killed him. Currently, the captain of the ship is fully in control of the ship, but we're part of a Tactical Unit headed to Garbon for drills. Once everything happened, we stood on standby, ready to assist the commander if necessary. When two of his men told us the pirates had killed him, we took over protecting the cockpit, and the captain was doing his best to get everyone to Garbon. They have the soldiers spread out, but a lot of them are no good since they have seen no type of warfare."

"I guess that's how they got out of that room. Do you know where they are now?" I wasn't going to let some tactical unit fail on killing them.

"We just got into a firefight with one of them. He ran off down the hallway. A couple of my soldiers chased after and I'm waiting for them to report back. Are you able to help us out? We don't need them to get to the cockpit at any cost. We have been given orders to kill any Deadly Cove pirates in this area." He spoke.

"I can help you out with that, but also, I'm searching for some females that might know them. The pirates might be after or collaborating with them. I don't know yet." He nodded, and I headed down the direction where his soldiers were. Another one of his soldiers led me just to let the other ones know who I was. This was going to be a lot more work than I thought.

SPARTEC

Flos Spacelines
Relax while we take you to your destination
Flos Spacelines
The best Space Service in the Neetoi Galaxy
We travel to near galaxies also for the Neetoi Galaxy. Check us out on the space web!

www.ingramcontent.com/pod-product-compliance
Lightning Source LLC
Chambersburg PA
CBHW042137120726
47911CB00022B/112